# ANIMAL POEMS

## Illustrated by Stephen Cartwright

## Selected by Heather Amery

Poems by

Tony Charles, Pie Corbett, Peter Dixon, Gina Douthwaite,
John Foster, David Harmer, Libby Houston, Michael Johnson,
Shelagh McGee, Robin Mellor, Trevor Millum, Judith Nicholls,
Julie O'Callaghan, Irene Rawnsley, Vernon Scannell,
Matt Simpson, Matthew Sweeney, Charles Thomson.

With thanks to Lois Beeson

## A Twentieth-Century Fox

The field is a pool of silver
a bright disc cut by the moon.

A grinning star
steps into the spotlight.

His woodland audience are tense
hold their breath, close their eyes.

They wish he would disappear
vanish like Dracula into his coffin.

But he begins to strut and dance
caper around on neat black feet.

His ginger wig and savage mask
disguise his eyes in the moonlight.

He relaxes, enjoys his act
scaring the audience to death.

*David Harmer*

## Algy Met a Bear

Algy met a bear,
A bear met Algy.
The bear was bulgy,
The bulge was Algy.

*Anon*

2

## Please, Noah!

### Tortoise

I'm slow, Noah,
slow.
Don't put me near the hare,
the horse's hoof,
the elephant.
I fear . . .
the python, Noah;
his curling tongue
is long enough
to pierce my home.
Let me share my room
with mole, light-footed wren
or snail; he cannot stamp
or run. Best of all,
just let me be
alone.

### Mouse

Am I the smallest, Noah?
Is it a trap?
Please, I'd like
cheese to gnaw
and nuts to nibble.
I won't quibble
if I have to share
with gerbil, guinea pig
or even rabbit, hare . . .
but please, not *cat*!
Dear Noah,
whatever else,
not *that*!

### Sloth

Sleep, Noah,
about my sleep.
I see it's going to be
quite hard for me
to sleep at sea.

You realize, Noah,
for a sloth,

just how important
sleeping is?
Both night
and day!
In fact,
I'd say
. . .
zzzzzzz

*Judith Nicholls*

3

## Happy Dogday

Today –
Is our dog's birthday.

It's Happydogdayday.
Sixteen years of panting
And sixteen years of play.

Sixteen years of dogtime.
Sixteen years of barks
– eating smelly dog food
And making muddy marks.

It's a hundred years of our time.
It's a hundred human years
– of digging in the garden
And scratching itchy ears.

A hundred years of living rooms
(he never goes upstairs)
and dropping hairy whiskers
And being pushed off chairs . . .

It's a hundred years of being with us
A hundred years of Dad . . .
And a hundred of my sister
(that must be really bad!)

So:

No wonder he looks really old
No wonder he is grey
And cannot hear
Or jump
Or catch
Or even run away . . .
No wonder that he sleeps all day
No wonder that he's fat
And only dreams of catching things
And chasing neighbours' cats . . .

So fight your fights
In dogdream nights
Deep within your bed . . .

today's your day
and we all say . . .

**Happy Birthday FRED!**

*Peter Dixon*

4

## Lion

Great rag bag
jumble headed thing
shakes its mane
in a yawn that turns to anger,
teeth picked out like stalactites
in some vast cave
bone grinders, flesh rippers
hyena bringers, jackal callers
and huge paws
the size of death
clamp down on antelope,
later, sleeping through the night
each star a lion
flung with pride across a sky
black as a roaring mouth
lion dreams of open spaces
dreams the smell of freedom.

*David Harmer*

## Caterpillar v Snail

Starts fast
legs ache . . .
Cabbage leaf,
quick break!
Eat much,
warm sun . . .
Snail's passed,
SNAIL WON!

One foot
starts slow.
Long way.
Food? No!
Keep on,
snail's pace.
Slowcoach
WINS RACE!

*Judith Nicholls*

## Sick as a Parrot

This parrot is not a nice bird,
It is spiteful and moody and red.
Its eyes are hot and flash a lot
In its bird-brained little head.

This parrot is not a pretty bird,
Its feathers are dusty and sad,
Its tail is green without any sheen
And its dandruff is awfully bad.

This parrot is not entertaining,
Doesn't sing, doesn't dance, doesn't speak.
It just sits and stares and mutters and glares
And hammers its perch with its beak.

This parrot belonged to grandad,
It chattered all day by his side,
It used to recite Old King Cole every night
But it's dumbstruck since grandad has died.

*Shelagh McGee*

## The Codfish

The codfish lays ten thousand eggs,
    The homely hen lays one.
The codfish never cackles
    To tell you what she's done.
And so we scorn the codfish,
    While the humble hen we prize,
Which only goes to show you
    That it pays to advertise.

*Anon*

## My Dear Pet

My baby rhino
is a playful little mite.
I ask her to stamp on my pastry dough
with her round flat foot.
Then I fill the footprint
with apples and raisins and cinnamon
and we have a party
with Hawaiian Punch
and apple pie covered in cream.
I know everyone boasts
about their singing turtles
and dancing stick insects
like they were hot stuff.
I don't care
because I've got a proud feeling
about my rhino.
So do you want to know her name?
I say to her, "Rosie, sit still
and stop trotting through the park –
these children want to see
what an ideal rhino you are."
She tickles me with her velvet ears
when I'm grumpy.
That's when she thinks
I'm her human pet.

*Julie O'Callaghan*

## News of the Python

Leopards tussled.
Monkeys flew.
The python breathed.

Water bubbled.
Storm-gusts grew.
The python breathed.

Ice-cream tumbled.
Paper blew.
The python breathed.

Easter Sunday
At the zoo:
The python breathed.

*Libby Houston*

## Bear Clothes

A Polar Bear's coat
buttons up to his throat
to keep out the cold
and snow.

A Polar Bear's scarf
would make you laugh
for he ties it up
in a bow.

A Polar Bear's boots
are useful on routes
for making his insides
glow.

But when it is hot
he wears what he's got,
a bare Bear from head
to toe.

*Pie Corbett*

## Animals in the Zoo Are Like People

I liked the cheeky chimpanzee –
my brother said it looked like me.

So I replied, "Your head's the shape
of that old, big old, fat old ape!"

He said, "Just look at that baboon –
it's got a face like Auntie June!!"

We stood right by the lion's cage:
it roared like dad does in a rage,

and then it lay down in a heap
like dad does when he goes to sleep.

And mum is like a kangaroo –
her apron's got a pocket too.

We saw a hippopotamus
(Gran said to Grandad, "Looks like us!").

But tell me, out of every creature,
which was the one that looked like teacher?

And lastly, out of all the zoo,
which was the one that looked like YOU?

*Charles Thomson*

# Fishbones Dreaming

Fishbones lay in the smelly bin.
He was a head, a backbone and a tail.
Soon the cats would be in for him.

He didn't like to be this way.
He shut his eyes and dreamed back.

Back to when he was fat, and hot on a plate.
Beside green beans, with lemon juice
squeezed on him. And a man
with a knife and fork raised, about to eat him.

He didn't like to be this way.
He shut his eyes and dreamed back.

Back to when he was squirming in a net,
with thousands of other fish, on the deck of a boat.
And the rain falling wasn't wet enough to breathe in.

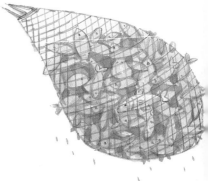

He didn't like to be this way.
He shut his eyes and dreamed back.

Back to when he was darting through the sea,
past crabs and jellyfish, and others like himself.
Or surfacing to jump for flies
and feel the sun on his face.

He liked to be this way.
He dreamed hard to try and stay there.

*Matthew Sweeney*

10

## Watercat

Our cat used to like water.
If Dad set up the sprinkler
he'd come in wet through
from leaping after
fountains in the air;

and he liked the aquarium,
would balance on the rim
trying to hook fishes,
until one day he fell in
and had to be rescued.

He lost interest then.
When he notices now
the flash of fish at play
he settles down on the rug,
facing the other way.

*Irene Rawnsley*

## Song-Thrush

Slug-slayer, snail-snatcher,
soprano turned percussionist,
mad drummer of the rock;
now executioner,
still centre-stage,
beats out her dizzy solo
on execution block.

*Judith Nicholls*

## Dog's Life

I don't like being me sometimes
        slumped here
on the carpet, cocking my ears
        every time
someone shuffles or shifts their feet
        thinking
could be I'm going walkies or getting grub
        or allowed
to see if the cat's left more than a smell
        on her plate.
She's never refused, that cat! Sometimes
        I find myself
dreaming – twitching my fur, my ears – of
        being just
say *half* as canny as her, with her pert miaow,
        her cheeky tail
flaunting! These people sprawled
        in armchairs
gawping at telly, why don't they play ball
        with me
or enjoy a good nose-licking, eh?

*Matt Simpson*

## If You Should Meet a Crocodile

If you should meet a crocodile,
   Don't take a stick and poke him;
Ignore the welcome in his smile,
   Be careful not to stroke him.

For as he sleeps upon the Nile,
   He thinner gets and thinner;
And whene'er you meet a crocodile
   He's ready for his dinner.

*Anon*

12

## Dancing the Anaconda

A n a c o n d a
starts to "Conga"! through a jungle (not the Congo).
Twisting round, along, then round, branch and
bough are danced around;
so smooth, except a bulge or two, where a
not-so-quick-step bird (or beast) or two, groove
to a graver tune.
A n a c o n d a
hokey-cokeys quite a few.

A n a c o n d a
growing longer.
Rivers offer no restriction to choreography's
constriction; the list of practised tactics
includes ballet aquatic.
"Come, we conga like a conger to apocalypso frogs,
or maybe rumba numbers that bop Orinoco hogs."

If you hear nocturnal rocking, when snake
charmers should be curling tight, it could be
A n a c o n d a
sleepwaltzing through those tango-tangled
forests of the night.

"Excuse me" for a danceclass treat, as
F r e d
and
G i n g e r
A n a c o n d a
meet.
(They never tread on one another's feet.)

*Mike Johnson*

13

## Alligator in the Zoo

A long slow line of leather
green and brown, all but dead.

A razor smile of icy teeth
a broad corrugated back

as tough as bark, like tree trunk
half-submerged by water.

Above the jaws set like traps
fathers dangle their babies' legs.

Dragon breath is smouldering
bubbling up from the snout.

One dropped shoe or careless kick
one brief sag of aching arms

and that huge mouth
will split apart like a flick-knife

snap the prey up
like a trout traps a fly.

*David Harmer*

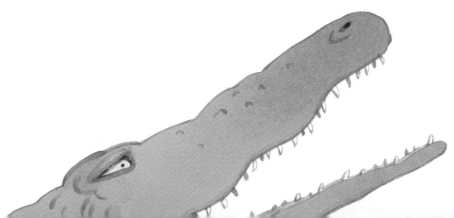

## The Purpose of Keeping a Tortoise

A tortoise
is not a pet I long to keep.
In Summer?
All he does is eat and crawl.
In Winter?
Hide and sleep!

*Judith Nicholls*

## Natty Bats

weird world of hi-fi echoes
they flittermouse around

fishing with their ultra-ears
for food in nets of sound

well-fed suspended from their toes

natty bats sleep upside-down!

*Mike Johnson*

## The Ptarmigan

The ptarmigan is strange,
As strange as he can be;
Never sits on the ptelephone poles
Or roosts upon a ptree.
And the way he ptakes pto spelling
Is the strangest thing pto me.

*Anon*

15

## The Dragon

Underneath our teapot stand,
in a small, compacted world
of dry dropped tealeaves,
a sulky dragon sleeps.

He wakens every once a while
for maidens from the biscuit tin
to bring him Current Crisp crumbs
or broken Garabaldis.

How he longs to see a shining knight
ride into his lonely kingdom,
with a coloured shield and flashing sword,
to remind him of the old days.

I would go and play with him
and cheer his melancholy,
and I would help the maidens fair
carry their gifts to his castle, but

*I'm not supposed to know he's there.*

*Robin Mellor*

## There Was a Small Maiden Named Maggie

There was a small maiden named Maggie,
Whose dog was enormous and shaggy;
The front end of him
Looked vicious and grim –
But the tail end was friendly and waggy.

*Anon*

16

## The Whalig and His Ele-Friend

Rasher the pig met Cutlet the calf
not knowing how lucky they were
             by half.

Of Rasher, his rear was rounded and pink,
with flickers of blotches like blotted black ink,
that came to an end in a question-mark tail.
The question was was he a pig, or a whale?
For Rasher, up front, was really a teaser –

no trotters, no snout, and he spouted a geyser
from in-between where his ears should have sprung.
This *whalig*, to market, should never have come
for there wasn't a farmer, nor butcher, would buy
as *whaligs* won't breed and *whaligs* won't fry!

But Rasher got shot in a photograph
not knowing how lucky he was
             by half.

Now Cutlet the calf had sugar brown eyes,
a wet leather nose and ears twice the size
of her sandpaper tongue that sucked, as a thumb,
(what else can a calf do when taken from mum?)
the end of her tail which was whippy and grey

till, ropy and wet, it started to fray
and straggle in strands down her baggy back end.
Cutlet, the calf, *whalig's* strange *ele-friend,*
was suitable neither for veal nor for hunting
which went in her favour – there had to be something!

So Cutlet and Rasher had the last laugh
not knowing how lucky they were
             by half.

*Gina Douthwaite*

## Cat

Cat's sneaky,
leaps on to my lap
with sudden claws
like nettle stings.

And now she is
tucking herself away –
O so tidily – right down to
her Chinese eyes.

Purrs like a lawnmower . . .
Yes, but her ears, her ears
are watching something

that hops and twitters
worm-hungry,
among the wet petunias.

*Matt Simpson*

## The Pelican

What a wonderful beast is the Pelican!
Whose bill can hold more than his belican.
    He can take in his beak
    Enough food for a week –
      And I'm damned
        if I know
          how the helican.

*Anon*

## My Dog

My dog belongs to no known breed,
A bit of this and that.
His head looks like a small haystack
He's lazy, smelly, fat.

If I say, "Sit!", he walks away.
When I throw stick or ball
He flops down in the grass as if
He had no legs at all,

And looks at me with eyes that say,
"You threw the thing, not me.
You want it back, then get it back.
Fair's fair, you must agree."

He is a thief. Last week but one
He stole the Sunday Roast
And showed no guilt at all as we
Sat down to beans on toast.

The only time I saw him run —
And he went like a flash —
Was when a mugger in the park
Tried to steal my cash.

My loyal, brave companion flew
Like a missile to the gate
And didn't stop till safely home.
He left me to my fate.

And would I swap him for a dog
Obedient, clean and good,
An honest, faithful, lively chap?
Oh boy, I would! I would!

*Vernon Scannell*

19

## Ten Dancing Dinosaurs

Ten dancing dinosaurs in a chorus line
One fell and split her skirt, then there were nine.

Nine dancing dinosaurs at a village fête
One was raffled as a prize, then there were eight.

Eight dancing dinosaurs on a pier in Devon
One fell overboard, then there were seven.

Seven dancing dinosaurs performing magic tricks
One did a vanishing act, then there were six.

Six dancing dinosaurs learning how to jive
One got twisted in a knot, then there were five.

Five dancing dinosaurs gyrating on the floor
One crashed through the floorboards, then there were four.

Four dancing dinosaurs waltzing in the sea
A mermaid kidnapped one, then there were three.

Three dancing dinosaurs head-banging in a zoo
One knocked himself out, then there were two.

Two dancing dinosaurs rocking round the sun
One collapsed from sunstroke, then there was one.

One dancing dinosaur hijacked a plane
Flew off to Alaska and was never seen again!

*John Foster*

# The Car Park Cat

```
      △                    K
   E    C              R    C
   H    A              A    A
   T    R              P    T
```

Car bonnet cat
keeping warm, car bonnet cat
with crocodile yawn, stares from his sand-
peppered forest of fluff, segment-of-lemon eyes warning,
*ENOUGH!* Just draw back that hand, retreat, *GO AWAY!*
and his claws flex a tune to say: I won't play but I'll spit
like the sea whipped wild in a gale, hump up like a wave,
flick a forked lightning tail, lash out and scratch at
your lobster-pink face, for no one, *but no one,*
removes from this place, car bonnet cat
keeping warm, car bonnet cat
by the name of
*STORM.*

*Gina Douthwaite*

## Goldfish Lament

I'm a goldfish
  a cold fish,
  a put-me-in-a-bowl fish —
    *where am I going to go?*

I'd like to be an old fish
  I've told fish,
  but now that I'm a sold fish
    *I fear that won't be so.*

*Judith Nicholls*

# Hammy's House

Jane nextdoor
has gone to Spain;
they wouldn't let her
take a hamster on the plane
so we're looking after him.

But the cage she brought
was cramped and small;
he scarcely had room
to move at all,
just a wheel, a dish and straw.

Dad said,
"He's got no room to play!
This hamster's
supposed to be on holiday.
Let's give him a surprise!"

He searched the garage
that very day
for the old doll's house
we'd thrown away,
mended the broken hinges,

put nuts inside,
screwed the wheel in place,
found fresh straw
for his sleeping space,
then popped him through the door.

Now he's busy
arranging his nest,
sorting his nuts out,
finding the best
to store in his bedroom,

working out on the wheel
of his gymnasium;
he'll not want to go back
when Jane comes home.
Maybe she'll let us keep him.

*Irene Rawnsley*

26

# There Wasn't a Shark at London Zoo

We saw a monkey coloured blue
but there wasn't a shark at London Zoo.

We saw the gorillas do kung fu
but there wasn't a shark at London Zoo.

We saw a leap-frogging kangaroo
but there wasn't a shark at London Zoo.

We saw some pigs (and what a pooh!)
but there wasn't a shark at London Zoo.

There were elephants there and lions too
but there wasn't a shark at London Zoo.

There were antelopes and a caribou
but there wasn't a shark at London Zoo.

We even joined a massive queue
but there wasn't a shark at London Zoo.

*Question*

Is it really, really, really true
that there isn't a shark at London Zoo?*

*"Oh no, there isn't a shark – we've got a
dogfish." I was told. I wonder if a dogfish
can bark underwater?

*Charles Thomson*

27

# The Camel's Hump

What's in the hump's a mystery
unparalleled in history.
Some say it's there for food and so on –
what evidence have they to go on?
I think it's like an empty tin
which he keeps bits and pieces in
*(and how does a camel keep up his hump?*
*He blows it up with a bicycle pump!)*

The proof for this is quite immense
if we apply some common sense,
so first let's answer this enquiry –
where does a camel keep his diary?
Not in a drawer, or on a rack
but tucked up safely on his back
*(and how does a camel keep up his hump?*
*He blows it up with a bicycle pump!)*

Where does he store away utensils?
Where does he put his pen and pencils?
Where does he keep his watch all night?
They're hidden safely out of sight,
not in a bag or plastic sack
but in the bump upon his back.
*(and how does a camel keep up his hump?*
*He blows it up with a bicycle pump!)*

*Charles Thomson*

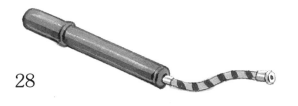

28

## Spider

Every morning at my sink
a spider crawls down for a drink.
She abseils from the window-sill
then folds up, keeping very still
until she thinks I've gone away
then
*one* leg,
*two* legs,
feel their way.
They prod, they probe,
legs *three*
and *four*
join in the fun. Then even more!
Legs *five*
and *six*
extend and lift
hydraulically – she tilts a bit
till hairy members
*seven*
and *eight*
receive their message, "*ACTIVATE*".
And so, across the soapy trickle,
she *flits*! – black threads of silky tickle –
till tidal waves, tipped from the bowl,
send her whirlpooling down the hole
\* \* \* \* \* \*
then
*one* leg,
*two* legs,
feel their way . . .

*Gina Douthwaite*

29

# Wanted – a Witch's Cat

Wanted – a witch's cat.
Must have vigour and spite,
Be expert at hissing,
And good in a fight,
And have balance and poise
On a broomstick at night.

Wanted – a witch's cat.
Must have hypnotic eyes
To tantalize victims
And mesmerize spies,
And be an adept
At scanning the skies.

Wanted – a witch's cat.
With a sly, cunning smile,
A knowledge of spells
And a good deal of guile,
With a fairly hot temper
And plenty of bile.

Wanted – a witch's cat,
Who's not afraid to fly,
For a cat with strong nerves
The salary's high
Wanted – a witch's cat;
Only the best need apply.

*Shelagh McGee*

## The Mouse and the Xmas Tree

The mouse ran up the Xmas tree
    hey ho, hey ho,
through a well-lit, uphill forest
    that wasn't there before
and he thought: all these bells
and stars, and deer, and dwarves
    are brill and honey-dandy
and I'll nibble some to prove it
but as I alone can climb the tree
    I am still the best.

And through the tree's green needles
    came the mouse's song:
*Hey ho, hey ho,*
*I'm fed up with the floor.*
*I'm even more bored*
    *with the world behind*
    *the skirting-board.*
*I like this stood-up wood.*

And he ran on up that Xmas tree
    as fast as he could
and the lights burned his sides
the needles pricked his fur
the bells blocked his way
but still he reached the top
where the angel was waiting
    to kick him, squealing,
    hey ho, hey ho,
    bumpety, scratchety, plop
on to the needle-strewn floor
where he'd been before,
    and where he'd stay.

*Matthew Sweeney*

# Index of first lines

Algy met a bear, 2
A long slow line of leather, 14
A n a c o n d a, 13
A Polar Bear's coat, 8
A tortoise, 15
Car bonnet cat, 25
Cat's sneaky, 18
Cecil the spider –, 21
Every morning at my sink, 29
Fishbones lay in the smelly bin, 10
Great rag bag, 5
I don't like being me sometimes, 12
If a hundred elephants, 22
If you should meet a crocodile, 12
I liked the cheeky chimpanzees –, 9
I'm a goldfish, 25
I'm slow, Noah, 3
Jane nextdoor, 26
Leopards tussled, 8
My baby rhino, 7
My dog belongs to no known breed, 19
Once upon a faraway time, 20

Our cat used to like water, 11
Rasher the pig met Cutlet the calf, 17
Slug-slayer, snail-snatcher, 11
Starts fast, 5
Ten dancing dinosaurs in a chorus line, 24
The codfish lays ten thousand eggs, 6
The field is a pool of silver, 2
The mouse ran up the Xmas tree, 31
The ptarmigan is strange, 15
There's a three-toed sloth in my apple tree: 23
There was a small maiden named Maggie, 16
This parrot is not a nice bird, 6
Today –, 4
Underneath our teapot stand, 16
Wanted – a witch's cat, 30
weird world of hi-fi echoes, 15
We saw a monkey coloured blue, 27
What a wonderful beast is the Pelican!, 19
What's in the hump's a mystery, 28

The publishers wish to thank the following for permission to reproduce the poems in this book:
Tony Charles for "Sloth"; Pie Corbett for "Bear Clothes"; Peter Dixon for "Happy Dogday";
Gina Douthwaite for "Spider", "The Car Park Cat", "The Whalig and His Ele-Friend"; John
Foster for "Ten Dancing Dinosaurs"; David Harmer for "Alligator in the Zoo", "Lion", "A
Twentieth-Century Fox"; Libby Houston for "News of the Python"; Mike Johnson for "Natty
Bats", "Dancing the Anaconda"; Shelagh McGee for "Wanted – a Witch's Cat", "Sick as a
Parrot"; Robin Mellor for "The Dragon"; Trevor Millum for "Cecil and the Widow"; Judith
Nicholls for "Goldfish Lament", "The Purpose of Keeping a Tortoise", "Song-Thrush",
"Caterpillar v. Snail", "Please, Noah!"; Julie O'Callaghan for "My Dear Pet"; Irene Rawnsley for
"Hammy's House", "Elephants", "Watercat"; Vernon Scannell for "My Dog"; Matt Simpson for
"Cat", "Dog's Life"; Matthew Sweeney for "The Mouse and the Xmas Tree", "Fishbones
Dreaming"; Charles Thomson for "The Camel's Hump", "There Wasn't a Shark at London
Zoo", "Animals in the Zoo Are Like People"

First published in 1990. Usborne Publishing Limited, 83-85 Saffron Hill, London EC1N 8RT,
England. This collection © Usborne Publishing Ltd. 1990. The individual copyrights belong to
the authors. The illustrations © Usborne Publishing Ltd. 1990. The name Usborne and the device
⁓ are Trade Marks of Usborne Publishing Ltd. All rights reserved. No part of this publication
may be stored in a retrieval system or transmitted in any form or by any means, electronic,
mechanical, photocopy, recording or otherwise, without the prior permission of the publisher.
Printed in Belgium.